Graveyard Scavenger Hunt

by

Brian Barnett

GRAVEYARD SCAVENGER HUNT
COPYRIGHT 2012 by Brian Barnett

Publishing History, Second Edition

Dedication

For Michael, Sebastian, Jane and Alex.

Chapter One

Plot after plot of farmland swished past. There was no other scenery save for the continuous stretch of flat fields sparsely filled with rolls of hay and the occasional black or red barn. Pete sighed and leaned forward. "How much longer is it?"

His mother glared in the rearview mirror. "I've told you twice already. It's just a few miles from the highway. We have maybe five more minutes or so before we get to your grandparents'."

Pete threw himself back into the seat and groaned as the seatbelt tightened. He pulled, trying to loosen it, but it refused to budge. "And *why* do I have to go?"

"I've told you *ten* times already, Pete. Your dad and I won a cruise in the Caribbean. We couldn't trade in the prize, and there was nobody else available to watch you on such short notice."

"I still don't see why they can't come to our house. I mean, I don't want to be dumped off in the middle of nowhere. Besides, I haven't seen them in years. I doubt they even want me there."

"Stop with that nonsense! They love you and are thrilled you're coming for a long overdue visit."

"Yeah right," he mumbled, staring at his reflection in the window. Narrowed blue eyes were almost a mirror image of his mother's while the sandy hair hanging over his wrinkled forehead was exactly like his father's.

"There it is." Pete's mother pointed.

"Where?" He hoped the house was hidden somewhere in the clumps of trees dotting the property and wasn't the dilapidated gray structure on the hill that had to be a mile from the road.

"The only place in sight, silly."

Pete's heart dropped. Of course the house would be musty and old. He bet it was full of spiders. He hated spiders.

Pete's mom turned onto an uneven gravel driveway pocked with deep potholes and irregular patches of weeds. A rotten wood mailbox leaned away from the road.

To the left of the ancient home were two large animal pens. One contained cows, and the other had goats. Several chickens poked around the yard. A faded red barn stood behind the house. Most of the property had tall, shin-deep grass, but near the house, the lawn was freshly mowed in neat diagonal rows, not that it helped the looks of the place.

The car jerked to the left, and Pete's head banged against the window. "Ow!"

"Sorry," his mother said. "I found a pothole, I guess."

"I guess," he muttered as he rubbed his throbbing forehead. A round, oily spot now decorated the window.

Pete sighed again. The driveway went on forever. It didn't help any that his mother drove slowly. *Most likely to avoid the other potholes.*

"I think your papaw and mamaw are going to be happy to see you. Heck, they've probably forgotten what you look like."

"So why would they be happy to see me then?" he grumbled.

"Just give them a chance, Pete. I'm sure they'll enjoy your company."

"Right. Then why doesn't Dad ever come to see them? They're *his* parents."

"They live way out here, and you know your dad. He stays so busy. Plus he calls them all the time."

"Well then maybe they should leave the house every once in a while. Do they know it is actually *normal* for people to own cars and TVs?" He folded his arms and stared across the grassy field. *Is that a gravestone?* "No way!"

"What?" The car lurched.

Pete pointed. "They actually have a graveyard next to their house? You never told me that! That's just sick!"

"Don't be silly, Pete. They've lived here for years, yet nothing has happened to them. Don't you think that if the graveyard was dangerous they would have moved away by now?"

Pete clenched his jaw so hard his teeth hurt. His heart pounded a few beats faster as he kept his gaze glued on the graveyard, watching for even a single blade of grass to go out of place. He looked away when they rolled to a stop near the front porch.

"We're here." Pete's mother flashed a perky smile toward him.

He rolled his eyes before climbing out to stretch his tired legs. They'd been driving forever. He yawned, moaning loudly until he clamped his jaw shut.

He walked to the trunk, where his mom struggled to lift two large suitcases. He took one and nearly dropped it. It was much heavier than he'd expected. Earlier, his dad had made the suitcase look so easy to load.

He trailed his gaze slowly to the graveyard. A chill crept over him as if hundreds of spiders prickled his skin. The gravestones were as gray and dingy as the house. Some of them stood crooked with large chunks missing. A black wrought-iron fence imprisoned the plots. Tall grass poked through the bars like it wanted to escape. Unease crawled up Pete's spine. Everything was quiet. Even the breeze was silent. *Something bad is going to happen.*

Knocking startled him, and he flinched. The pace of his heart doubled. Still peering at the graveyard, he inched toward the house.

Pete climbed the splintering porch stairs. They creaked under his weight. Afraid at any moment he might fall through the rotten planks, he put down the heavy suitcase and slid it away with his foot. The wood groaned under its weight.

"Mom, can we go?" He whispered, tugging her shirt sleeve.

"Now don't start, Pete." She pulled her arm free and knocked again, setting the other suitcase on the porch.

"Maybe they're not home," Pete said hopefully.

"No. They said they would be here. Your mamaw is just hard of hearing." She knocked a little harder. Gray paint chips flaked off the wooden screen door.

"Who's doing all that banging?" a deep voice boomed from the far end of the porch.

Startled, Pete stepped back and tripped over a suitcase, which then fell open. A sudden stiff breeze picked up the clothes and sent them tumbling across the dusty driveway. He fumbled to catch the nearest pieces before glancing toward the far end of the porch.

A wiry old man with a meat cleaver stood wearing a tattered white smock. The cleaver and smock were both covered with something bright and red, like fresh blood. Pete's knees went weak, and fear clawed up his throat.

Chapter Two

"Hi, Orville," Pete's mom called.

Orville laughed until tears formed in his eyes. His large smile exposed several missing teeth. "Oh Pete, you should've seen your face," he said, slapping his knee. He sucked in a desperate breath then continued to laugh some more.

Pete stared at the man who wore the bright red-stained apron and held a meat cleaver with shimmering red film covering the blade. Was this man really his papaw? Had the man lost his mind? What was with all the blood?

"You two having trouble getting into the house?" Orville asked. He peeked at Pete and chuckled, shaking his head.

"Yeah, I've been knocking for a few minutes now, but nobody has answered. Is Lidia okay?" Pete's mother asked.

"Oh yeah. She's almost as deaf as a post." He unlatched the door then kicked it. It swung open with a loud *bang*, and a faint shriek came from a back room. Orville shot Pete another toothless grin.

Over Orville's shoulder, Pete saw an old lady with a head full of curly gray hair poke her head around an entryway that he guessed was to the kitchen, given the dark, wood grain cabinets hanging on the wall. Her eyes were wide, and her mouth was half open. The door slowly swung closed, blocking Pete's view.

"Hey, old woman!" Orville called, pushing his way back through the door. "This young man wants to stay with us for a while. Is that okay with you?" He chortled and motioned for Pete and his mom to follow.

Pete scanned the interior of the house. It was as old and splintery inside as it was out. The main hall was a large space with wood paneling. No pictures were hung, and only one chair stood against the wall next to the open back door. To the right, a staircase with flaking white paint led to a dark second floor. His gaze moved to a dusty, cheap-looking chandelier that barely gave off light.

"Well, look how grown up he is!" Mamaw yelled from the kitchen to his left. "I remember when you were only just yay-high." She held her hand about three feet from the ground. "You used to run around with your hair just a-flyin'. Heck, we still have some old clothes your parents left. I doubt they'd fit you now, though." She laughed breathily.

Not remembering those times, Pete smiled awkwardly and nodded. "Yeah, I've done a lot of growing up, I guess."

"You bet ya! I hate to part with good company, but these potatoes aren't going to peel themselves!" she said before disappearing into the kitchen.

"Have you been working, Orville?" Pete's mom gestured toward the back door.

About fifty yards behind the house, the barn's large wooden doors stood open, revealing creepy, jagged shadows of who knew what. Pete shuddered as a cold chill ran up his spine. *No way I'm ever going in there.*

"Huh?" Orville looked blank for a moment before his expression cleared. "Oh, yes. Sorry about the mess. I had better get cleaned up." He spun to Pete and raised the cleaver high. "Aaah!"

Pete jumped backward, tripped and then fell against the door. Orville cackled all the way up the stairs and into whichever room he entered.

Pete stared at his mother until she turned and whispered, "He likes to play around. You'll get used to it."

"You've got to be kidding me! What's with all the blood? Is he a serial killer or something?" Pete whispered.

"He was probably just cutting up some supper when we got here."

Pete's stomach lurched. "Cutting up supper?"

"Yeah, probably chicken or beef. I don't remember if they've ever owned any pigs. I guess you'll find out."

"Oh man." Pete groaned. He wanted to go home, where he could eat a normal meal, like pizza or cheese-smothered nachos.

"You'll be just fine." She glanced at her watch and gasped. "Oh my! I need to go! I guess I've forgotten just how far this house is from town. We'll be leaving in a few hours." She grabbed Pete's face with both hands and put a big kiss on his forehead. "Now you be good and listen to what your papaw and mamaw say, okay?"

Pete sighed and wiped away the damp spot on his forehead. He hated it when she treated him like a baby.

She tilted his chin until their gazes met. "Okay?"

He groaned, rolling his eyes. "Okay."

She gave him a tight hug before leaving. "Oh Pete!" she called from the front porch.

Pete's heart leapt. Maybe she had decided to let him come along after all. Maybe she had changed her mind about going all together. He ran to the door. "Yeah?"

She stood by the suitcase that had fallen open earlier. "Pick up your clothes. They are going to be filthy after blowing across the driveway."

His stomach sank. She was really going to leave, and he was stuck here all alone.

She climbed in the car, started it and then turned it around. The tires crunched over the gravel as she drove away waving her arm out the window. The car lunged forward, and her arm disappeared back through the window.

Pete shook his head. *she must have driven into another pothole.*

His mom paused briefly at the end of the driveway and then turned onto the highway. In a matter of moments, she was gone.

Pete had never felt so stranded and alone in his whole life. He remembered other times he had watched her drive away, leaving him behind. His first day of school, last year during summer camp, neither compared to this.

He trudged to the edge of the porch. Clothes were scattered all the way to the driveway and blowing across the yard.

He gathered a few pairs of blue jeans that dangled on the bottom porch step. A shirt clung to a long-dead rosebush. Pete followed the trail of clothes around the side of the house. As he neared the graveyard, dread slowed his steps.

As if in a cruel joke, a shirt lay in the grass at the base of the wrought-iron fence surrounding the small graveyard. He walked over and dropped the other clothes on top of it to get a better hold on them all. Instead of picking the pile back up, he stood there, staring beyond the rusted fence.

Most of the grave plots were overgrown with weeds. Some of the headstones had crumbled to powder. Those still intact were grayed and cracked with age. The names and dates on the facings had eroded off long ago.

Then he saw them. A pair of boxers had somehow made their way into the graveyard. Pete's chest pounded as he crept toward the gate.

It's only a graveyard. It's only a graveyard.

He lifted the rusted latch. It made a metallic *screech* and reddish dust fell. Pete wiped his hand on his pants then pushed the gate open. The hinges squealed. Chills ran up Pete's spine. A sound like that could wake the—well, it was best not to think about what a sound like that could wake.

He crept beyond the gate, stepping lightly. *It's only a graveyard. It's only a graveyard.*

He wasn't sure why he was sneaking, but the graveyard felt like a forbidden place. Besides, it gave him the creeps. He had seen enough horror movies to know better than to just walk into a graveyard. At any moment, a skeletal hand could bust out of the ground and grab his ankle in a vice-like grip.

He shuddered. *It's only a graveyard! It's only a graveyard!*

Finally, he made it to the boxers. He looked around. Except for the occasional cricket chirp, it was quiet. He bent down and picked up the underwear.

His mother had bought them because she thought they were cute. There was nothing cute about them. They were dark blue with multi-colored smiley faces all over them. He tucked the boxers into his shirt, so his grandparents wouldn't see them. He didn't need those two laughing all week about a pair of stupid underwear.

A powerful hand, like the one he'd feared in his imagination, clamped down on his shoulder. There was no way to escape!

Chapter Three

"You shouldn't be here!"

Pete gasped. His heart leapt to his throat, trying to pound its way out. The grip on his shoulder loosened, and Pete spun to see Orville, who had changed into a red-checkered shirt and a pair of denim overalls.

"You shouldn't come in here, Pete," he said. "It's ... uh ... it can be dangerous after dark. You might trip and fall or something. Your mother would never forgive me if you were laid up with a head injury or a busted leg all week."

Pete slowed his breathing. "I was just getting some clothes that blew in here. I wasn't going to stay long."

Orville, who Pete decided to think of as Papaw to avoid any further awkwardness, narrowed his eyes as if he was suspicious. "I don't see any clothes. Are you sure you weren't just coming in here to mess around? This is no place to play, you know. Like I said, it's dangerous."

"The clothes are over by the fence."

"You said some blew in here."

Pete sighed then pulled the boxers from under his shirt. The bright green, red, yellow and blue smiling faces mocked him as he blushed.

"Well, aren't those snappy?" Papaw's face lightened as he chuckled. "Come on, let's get inside. The old lady has whipped up supper. You like hamburgers?"

They started toward the house. Of course he liked hamburgers. But then again, he had never thought about where they came from, until now. "Yeah, I guess so."

Papaw closed the screeching gate. His gaze darted from one end of the graveyard to the other before he turned away.

"Is everything okay?" Pete asked.

"Well, of course. What could be wrong?" Papaw forced a light chuckle.

"I don't know." Pete shrugged, glancing around. "You seem nervous about the graveyard, that's all."

Papaw was quiet for a few seconds. "Nah, I'm not nervous. There's nothing in there but dusty old bones, anyhow."

Pete was unconvinced. Papaw's uneasiness told him something was weird about it, but he let it go. Why make his papaw uncomfortable? He had to spend a whole week here. No reason to make it miserable for everybody.

"Listen." His tone serious, Papaw grabbed Pete's shoulders and stared into his eyes. "I don't want you messing around in the graveyard anymore this week, ya hear? It's no place to be playing. It can be—"

"Dangerous." Pete sighed.

"Yes, exactly. Don't you forget it either, okay?" Papaw patted Pete's shoulder and straightened.

Pete hated to be treated like a baby, and this was twice in one day. *I'm old enough to keep from hurting myself in a stupid, old graveyard.* "I won't go in there again."

They began walking back to the house. The wet grass clippings clung to their shoes. "You promise?"

"I promise."

"Okay then. You go on in, and I'll grab your clothes. And then let's get some eats!" Papaw flung open the front door with a *bang*. A faint yelp came from the kitchen.

He couldn't help but join his papaw in a laugh.

The house smelled great. It was as if the grease from hamburgers and French fries hung heavily in the air, just like the small diners his parents occasionally took him to. "Greasy spoons" was what they called the places.

Pete sat at the table in the center of the kitchen. An old refrigerator with a latch handle sat across the room. Dark wood cabinets lined most of the walls, except for where two windows opened to the property. One window had a view of the barn and the wooded area behind it. The other gave a view of the animal pens. Mamaw was at the stove. On the counter next to her was a platter with greasy hamburgers piled in a lumpy pyramid.

Papaw shook his head as he entered the room. "I put your clothes in your room." He glanced at Mamaw. "She takes forever sometimes." A smile formed on Papaw's face. "Watch this," he whispered. He crept right up behind Mamaw and turned, still smiling, toward Pete. His eyes lit up, and he nodded as if to say, "*Oh yeah. I'm going to get her.*"

Pete smiled but shook his head. Was Papaw going to hassle Mamaw the whole week?

Papaw jumped up and grabbed Mamaw's arms, snorting loudly.

"Oh!" She spun with a hand on her chest then slapped Papaw on the arm with a greasy spatula. "You're going to be the death of me, Orville!" She turned to Pete, half smiling. "He does this all the time. But I have to say, since you've come, he's gone from bad to worse. I guess he has someone to show off to now. Can you believe him?" She smacked Papaw's arm again.

"Oh lighten up, old woman." Papaw smiled and sat at the table.

Pete fiddled with his napkin. His grandparents seemed nice enough, but what was he supposed to talk about? Should he laugh at any of Papaw's practical jokes or not? He just wanted to go on to bed and sleep for a week. Then when he woke, he could go back home where he belonged.

Finally, Mamaw turned from the stove and scraped the contents of the skillet into a large bowl. "Have you ever had country fried potatoes?" she asked.

The potatoes and onions had turned brown, but they smelled terrific. Pete shook his head and took another deep sniff. The aroma stung his eyes and burned his nose, but there was something about it that made his mouth water. "Smells good," he said.

"Thanks! Do you want some milk?" she asked.

Though he really didn't, he said, "Sure." He just wanted to eat and drink the minimum he needed to survive and, afterward, leave so everyone could go about their normal life.

She poured milk from a white ceramic pitcher.

Pete took a quick drink and almost gagged. Had it spoiled? He couldn't bring himself to swallow. He spit it back into the cup.

"What's wrong?" Mamaw asked with a worried frown.

"I think this milk has gone bad." He held the glass up and tried to control his nausea.

She examined the glass, tilting it for a better look inside. "I collected it just this morning. There shouldn't be anything wrong with it at all." She sipped it.

He cringed. He hated to drink after people. There was no way he was going to finish the milk now.

She smacked her lips. "Tastes just fine to me." She licked away the thin white strip on her upper lip.

"That doesn't taste like any milk I've ever had." He grimaced. "What kind of cow has milk like that? What the heck did it eat?"

She laughed. Then Papaw laughed. They looked at each other and laughed even harder. She covered her mouth, and he slapped the table. Tears formed in the corners of her eyes.

What had he said to set them both off? He grew hot with embarrassment and frustration. "What? What's so funny?"

"The cows are for eating," she said through a broken laugh. "That's goat's milk."

Pete sighed. He had never wanted to go home so bad in all his life.

Chapter Four

After supper, Pete climbed the creaky stairs to the guest room. *What an event supper was.* He had never eaten such greasy hamburgers or even heard of country fried potatoes, though he admitted those were good. Never before had he tasted anything as vile and disgusting as goat's milk.

He looked forward to disappearing into his room. He opened the door then shook his head. It was barely a room at all. It was tiny and smelled faintly of dust. The patch-quilt-covered, twin bed took up most of the room, and a small dusty dresser, sitting in the corner, nearly took up the rest. The room was more like a broom closet.

He sat at the foot of the bed. The springs screeched. He looked out the window. The sky was turning orange and the canopies of the trees that lined the back of the property were getting darker by the second. Shadows stretched long and thin across the yard as the sun sank behind the house.

Something fluttered in the yard. *A piece of paper?* He strained his eyes. *Yes!* It *was* a piece of paper. Judging from its size, it was from his art book.

Pete loved to draw. The pad of art paper his mom had bought him for his twelfth birthday must have been packed in the suitcase that fell open. He must have missed it when picking up his stray clothes.

He groaned. "Aw, man." How many pages had he lost in the wind? There was no telling. Countless pictures that he had drawn were probably skittering across the countryside.

He hopped off the bed and ran into the hallway. His heavy footsteps shook the floorboards. He hurried down the stairs, each step bowing underfoot. Once he reached the bottom, he sprang for the door, yanked it open, and then leapt onto the porch.

Sure enough, several large sheets of paper, some with pictures, some without, were blowing across the yard. Despite not having caught his breath, he sighed hard.

Pete looked for the drawing pad. Why hadn't the paper blown around with the clothes? He spotted the pad that had been partially hidden under the porch. No wonder he had missed it earlier. It must've been shielded from most of the wind. He snatched it up then chased down the papers that had not yet been completely blown away.

He found a drawing of a monster truck. He had almost given up drawing it when he couldn't quite get the tires right. They had kept coming out crooked, but finally, after several tries, they turned out right. That was a very proud achievement for him.

He grabbed another sheet of paper that had a dinosaur with bloody teeth. He had drawn it a week ago, right before he heard he was going to have to stay with his grandparents. The blood was added after the news.

He found another sheet with a half-finished barn. He shoved into the notebook. "Stupid wind," he grumbled.

As far as he could tell, there was only one more sheet left to pick up. It was stuck in some tall weeds at the base of a cracked headstone.

It was a drawing of his dad. He had worked for weeks to get the shading just right. It still looked a little funny, but his dad loved it and said it had made him proud. Pete had to grab it before the wind swept it away.

With his hand on the latch of the wrought-iron gate, Pete paused. *Why had Papaw been so nervous about the graveyard?* Was there something to fear? *Ghosts? Ghouls? Goblins? How ridiculous.* Papaw was probably more afraid Pete would break an old family headstone or something.

Pete looked toward the house. He hoped he had not alerted his grandparents when he left the house. He'd made a lot of noise running down the stairs. There was no sign of them, so he continued. He climbed over the fence. It was be much quieter than using the gate and Papaw will never know he had even gone into the graveyard again.

Pete landed with a soft *thud* in the tall grass on the other side of the rusty fence. He jerked his head around and scanned the graveyard. Had he heard something on the opposite end? *It must've been the wind*. He hoped.

He snatched the drawing and studied the features of his dad's face. The shading on the chin still disappointed him. It looked like his dad had a crooked beard or something. What could he do to fix it? He held the paper closer, but the lighting was bad, so he tucked it into the pad.

Pete froze. What was that? There it was again. Someone had *grunted*.

Pete's heart raced. Nearly paralyzed with fear and breathless, he slowly scanned the tiny graveyard. Someone was inside it with him. But where?

The sun had dipped behind the house and everything was tinted a dark blue. The older, more crumbled headstones were nearly impossible to see now. Shadows shrouded everything.

"Hello?" Pete squeaked. Maybe it was Papaw about to play a practical joke to teach him a lesson. He should have listened to him in the first place. The graveyard *was* really dark at night. He actually *could* fall and hurt himself.

"Hello?" His voice cracked. Another grunt followed by dirt crumbling was all that answered. Who would be digging at this time of night? And why?

Pete strained his eyes but could see nothing but darkness. He stepped as silently as the crinkling grass and crunching dirt beneath his feet would allow. He went deeper into the graveyard, toward the sounds of digging and steady muffled grunts.

Pete reached the source of the sound. He dropped his art pad. Nobody was digging. At least, nobody was digging *into* a grave. Someone was digging out!

A bony hand burst upward from the ground, gripped the surrounding dirt and weeds, and pulled. Another grunt came from *within* the grave. Pete froze as rigid as a granite statue. People were supposed to stay buried!

A white face emerged. The skin was completely gone. A large worm wriggled from where an eye should've been. Pete's knees went so weak he had to grab onto a nearby headstone to keep from falling.

"Well kid, are you going to help me out of here, or not?"

Chapter Five

Despite the urge to run, Pete couldn't. His feet had taken root. He stared in disbelief at the skeleton clumsily climbing out of the grave.

The moon, directly overhead, dimly lit the scene. The skeleton wore a dark suit with light-colored pinstripes and black shoes dulled with mud. His jaw moved. "Thanks a lot, kid. Jeez." He bent down and pulled a grimy old hat from the hole. "Benny Barton's the name." He held out his fleshless hand. Tiny bits of debris fell from between the finger bones.

Pete continued to stare, wide-eyed, and did *not* offer his hand. *There is no way I'm talking to a skeleton right now.*

"Uh, well, most people around here just call me Bones. For obvious reasons, I suppose." He straightened his hat and brushed some of the excess roots, dirt, and bugs from his suit. "So, what's your name, kid?"

His suit fit very loosely. His shirt collar hung too low and his pants were extremely baggy. The way his jacket hung from his shoulders, reminded Pete of the times he would jokingly wear his dad's jacket. The shoulders were too wide for him and it looked a little like a shapeless blanket draped over his boney frame.

Benny grunted after the long wait and Pete snapped out of his stare. The last thing he wanted to do was to annoy the skeleton, so he stammered, "Uh, Pete. Pete Davidson, I mean."

"Well, it's a pleasure to meet you, Pete Davidson. So what all did Orville tell you about me? I'm sure he could go on for days. We go way back."

Was Benny the reason why Papaw had stared so uneasily at the graveyard? "No, I don't believe he mentioned you. Actually, I'm sure of it."

Benny shook his head. Another trail of dirt fell, this time from the hole where his nose should have been. "Well, ain't that a shame? We used to be buddies, him and me. You see, we used to play games together." Benny removed his hat and scratched his bony fingertips against his skull. It sounded like two clay pots grinding together. "Are you sure he didn't mention me?"

"Yep, I'm sure. Sorry." Pete offered a slight shrug. He was still shaken. How could a skeleton talk? Was it real? It shouldn't be possible, but it had to be. The cool wind on his face and the smell of dirt confirmed it was certainly no dream. But nothing good could come from a talking skeleton. He had to get away. He took a careful step backward. He didn't want to be noticed in mid-escape.

"Well, I guess it has been a while. Maybe he's forgotten about me." Benny's shoulders slumped a bit. "Oh well, I guess you and me can play. What do you say?"

Pete took another step back. His art pad still lay on the ground where he'd dropped it. He decided against reaching for it. Who knew what Benny was capable of? Maybe he was waiting for an opportunity to attack. If Pete bent down to pick up his art pad, then that would give Benny such an opportunity.

"So, how good are you at finding things?" Benny asked while looking at his fingertips as if he was about to groom non-existent fingernails.

Pete took another step back. *Time to make a run for it.* It was now or never.

"Hey, kid. Are you good at finding things or not?" Benny crossed his arms.

Pete turned to run but stopped cold. The wrought iron fence was gone. The *house* was gone.

For miles, there was nothing but rolling hills of tombstones, crypts and monuments—none of which had been there before. All along the hills were dead, twisted trees and ponds. The closest of the ponds were covered in moss and slime. All of it, every acre, had a sickly silver glow from the massive full moon.

Where am I? How in the world did I get here?

"Well, it looks like you don't have much of a choice now, huh?" said Benny.

"Where am I?" Pete asked shakily. "Where's my grandparents' house?"

Benny tilted his head a bit to the side. "You mean Orville is your grandfather?"

"Yeah ..." He was afraid to continue, unsure why Benny would care. "So?"

"So?" Benny chuckled. "So you came to challenge me after all these years. He must have told you about me after all! I guess you don't want to be shown up by your grandfather, and you came here to prove you're just as good as he was. Well, make no mistake, this time I will not be so easy to beat!"

"I told you already, he never told me about you!" Pete stomped his foot. "Now where am I, and how do I get home?"

Pete swore Benny smiled, even though he was nothing more than bones.

"You won't be able to go home until you beat me, which will be impossible, so you can pretty much forget about it."

Fear twinged within Pete's chest. He cleared the knot from his throat. "What do you mean by beat you?"

Benny clapped his bony hands together. "I get to go on another scavenger hunt! It's been years! Well, you should know. The last time I had one was when your grandfather beat me. The lucky devil. Well, mind you, not this time. No, sir!"

"A scavenger hunt? Are you serious?" The idea was completely absurd. Why would a skeleton challenge someone to a scavenger hunt? How could a skeleton even walk or talk in the first place?

"Well, of course. It wouldn't be very sporting of me to just bring all my friends back for no good reason. There are rules about such things, you know?"

"What friends?"

"Okay, let me lay this out for you. I'll say it nice and slow so your fleshy ears can catch it." Benny straightened his tattered tie and brushed away a centipede that climbed out of his jacket pocket. "You and I are going to play a little game. We will be going on a scavenger hunt. If I win, which I will, all of my friends will get to come back from their graves. You understand? This place is where the dead are kept. They want out, trust me. They want what they used to have."

Pete was suddenly nauseous. He'd never asked to join any stupid game, let alone deal with dead people. "You mean the dead will come back to life?"

"Well, not in the sense that you know it. We'll look pretty much like we do right now. But we'll live above ground. The world may get kind of crowded though. There are a lot more of us than there are of you folks. I can't even imagine the crime rate when some of these folks come back!" Benny laughed.

"So what happens if I win?"

"You won't, so don't worry about it."

Benny's playfulness frustrated Pete. "There's a chance I will! So what happens then?"

Benny sighed, a whistling sounded from where his throat should be. "Well, then we just stay the way we are, and you get to go home. But don't get your hopes up!"

Pete's knees weakened. The fate of the world rested on his shoulders. Losing was not an option.

Chapter Six

"Excuse me." A tiny voice startled Pete.

He turned to see a small man who stood maybe three-feet tall dressed in a black tuxedo. His oily, black hair was smoothed tightly against his scalp. He wore a monocle and had a pencil-thin mustache. He brushed by Pete and presented two rolled-up documents tied with red ribbons, one to Benny and the other to Pete.

"Okay, gentlemen," he said in a high-pitched voice. "I've just handed you your individual lists. Get to know them well. They are completely different from each other, so that no cheating by theft can occur." The little man narrowed his eyes at Benny.

Benny looked away, turning his attention to the stars while whistling an unfamiliar tune. If Benny had had skin, he would have been blushing.

Glancing at his list, Pete said, "Excuse me, sir."

"Yes, yes, what is it?" The little man sounded rather annoyed.

Pete looked at the little man. "Uh, I've never heard of some of this stuff. I don't even know where to start."

"Little boy, that is not my concern. I am here to act as a mediator. I couldn't care less whether or not you understand your list. My job is to present it to you and to make sure you have all the items listed when you claim that you have finished. Understood? If you have any other questions, please wait until I complete what I have to say!" The little man's tiny black eyes burned with fury.

Pete nodded, afraid of the man's temper. "Yes, sir."

"I don't like this list, Heikle," Benny whined. "Can we switch?"

"Listen, Bones, I will not tolerate your mischievous behavior again! Last time you cheated and stole your way through the game to get your items, and in the end you didn't even have the correct ones! One more insolent peep from you and this little contest is over before it begins, understood!"

Benny huffed and sat on a large rock.

"Now, where was I?" asked Heikle. "Oh, right. These lists were specifically chosen for the two of you. One list is for a novice, and the other is for someone who should know his way in and out of this place by now." Again, he eyed Benny.

Benny merely shrugged. Pete assumed that if the skeleton had eyes he would've rolled them.

Heikle turned to Pete. "Okay, young man, now do you have any questions?"

"Tons, I think." But Pete wasn't sure what to ask. The last thing he wanted was to get on Heikle's bad side. Heikle seemed to have an awful temper. Pete looked at his list, written in perfect cursive, read:

Wart of a Toad

Slime from Hanover's Pond
Dead Flowers from Mitchell's Tomb
Fresh Flies from Gaug's Den
Mud from Hudson Pond
A Spade from Ceryl's Shanty
Bark from Hangman's Tree
A Splinter from Dr. Kauffman's Coffin Lid
Rust from the Gate of Chaney's Crypt

"Okay, kid, spit it out already. What do you need to know?" Heikle huffed as he placed his tiny fists on his waist. His cheeks were bright red.

"Who's Gaug?"

Benny chuckled. His ribs clacked together.

"That's enough from you, Bones," said Heikle. "Gaug is our resident ghoul. He's rather ill-tempered. You'll do well if you avoid him altogether. He only goes in his den during the day. It's only light out for a few hours here. In fact, it'll be a good ten hours or more before the sun comes up. You shouldn't have to deal with him at all."

The nervous twinge returned to Pete's stomach. An ill-tempered ghoul? The scavenger hunt was not going to be easy.

"Are we about finished here?" asked Benny. "I'm starting to get arthritis with all this sitting around."

"Only as long as the rules are understood by everyone." Heikle glanced toward Pete. It was the first look of kindness Heikle had given since he showed.

"I guess they are. I just collect this stuff and bring it back to you as soon as possible, right?"

Heikle smiled and nodded. "You've got it. It couldn't be easier."

Pete couldn't help but think, easy to Heikle wasn't necessarily easy for everybody else.

Benny pushed off the rock and stretched. His joints popped and grinded. "Well, if you're ready, I am."

Pete's palms began to sweat. "I guess I am too." He glanced at his list. Perhaps it wouldn't be so hard. After all, Heikle said it was designed for a novice.

"I'll leave you two alone now," Heikle said while slowly dissolving into thin air. "No funny business!" Heikle's voice said as if from a distance.

Pete imagined Heikle was looking at Benny when he said it.

"Well, you heard him," said Benny. "I guess we had better be off."

Benny pointed beyond Pete's shoulder. "I think I need to head in this direction." He stepped quickly and bumped Pete's shoulder hard.

"Ouch!" Pete said, dropping his list.

Benny had dropped his too. Benny snatched them both up and handed one back to Pete. "Well, I'll see you around! Who knows, maybe I'll see you again before it's all over with." Benny took off running, his bones rattling and clacking together.

Pete rubbed his shoulder, which throbbed from the collision. It almost seemed as if Benny had rammed him on purpose. He looked at his list, and his heart sank. Benny had switched the lists! He must have planned it all along.

Pete looked around for Heikle, but he was long gone. Pete had no one to rely on but himself.

He read his new list, again in perfect cursive. It read:

A Twig from The Nearest Bush
A Straw from Dusty's Head
A Strand of Seaweed from Melvin's Pond
Hair from A Pig's Tail from Hilda's Hut
A Blue-Flamed Lantern from Cyril's Shanty
A Bone from Gaug's Scrap Pile

The list was slightly shorter than his old one. Perhaps it would be easier.

Gaug's name drew his gaze.

Heikle had said Gaug was one mean customer. Hopefully the scrap pile was located within Gaug's den. Pete hoped he could sneak in while it was still dark out. Otherwise he might have to deal with meeting Gaug after all. But there was no telling what other sorts of dangers lurked in the shadows of the endless graveyard.

From the distance Pete heard a faint "Woohoo!" Benny's cheer was enough to tell him he was already falling behind.

The fate of the world was in Pete's hands. It was time to do something about it, whether he was ready to or not.

Chapter Seven

"*Pssst*. Hey, kid."

Pete nearly jumped out of his skin. Wide-eyed, he looked around, yet there was nobody nearby.

"Hey you, kid, over here." The voice was barely a whisper. It didn't sound menacing, but in a place as strange as this giant graveyard, anything was possible.

Pete slowly turned. As far as he knew, the voice belonged to some sort of horrible goblin or a giant, man-eating troll. Still, there was nobody around.

"Yeah, that's it. Come here. Grab one of my twigs. You can do it."

Pete stepped forward, fully prepared to run if the situation called for it. "Hello?" Pete called, barely above a whisper. "Who's there?"

"Just keep walking and you'll find out soon enough."

Pete stopped, frozen in fear. Someone was definitely trying to get his attention, but there was nowhere for anyone to hide. There was only an old leafless bush, a few small gravestones and a thin tree nearby. "Just come over here, kid!"

"Where are you? I don't see you." Pete shuffled in the direction of the bush.

"I'm right in front of you, silly."

Maybe it was a ghost. "All I see is a bush." Then Pete remembered his list. The first item was a simple one, a twig from the nearest bush.

"That's right, kid. You've almost made it. Just a little further. I can give you a branch if you need one. Come on, I've got a lot of lovely twigs. All you have to do is ask me for one politely."

Pete stopped. "Wait! How did you know I need a twig?"

"I've been here for a very long time. I know how things work around here. Do you think you're the first to need a twig from me? I can assure you that you aren't. Not by a long shot."

The pit of his stomach burned. Who could be trusted? Most of the people in the graveyard were probably out to help Benny. It would definitely benefit them to do so.

He summoned the courage to speak again. "Show me your face. Then I'll talk to you. I don't have a lot of time to waste."

"I don't think you want to see my face."

"Fine, suit yourself. I've got work to do." Pete grabbed a rubbery twig, but instead of breaking loose, it bent and flexed like a pipe-cleaner. He sighed. If all the simple challenges were as difficult, it was going to be a long night.

Suddenly, the bush rattled. Its limbs vibrated, and its tinier branches loudly rustled against each other. Two branches whipped from underneath the bush and coiled around Pete's ankles. They tightened then yanked him off his feet.

Pete fell with a *thud* onto his back, knocking the wind from his lungs. While he struggled to catch his breath, the bush grew in size. It stood upright, towering over him. Its branches spread and separated to reveal a thin, wooden body.

After catching his breath, Pete focused on the bush-creature. Its face was hideous. It had two black eyes and a gaping mouth dribbling black sap from its wooden lips.

"I told you I would freely give you one of my twigs, but you insisted on trying to remove one manually. Why were you so arrogant as to deny my generous offer?"

Pete attempted to climb to his feet, but they were fastened together with ropey vines. The more he struggled, the tighter the restraints grew. Panic set in. "I'm sorry! I thought you were trying to trick me."

"Insolence! Why must you assume I was trying to trick you? Do you not understand the concept of respect?"

"Benny already tricked me once! I thought you were on his side. How was I supposed to know you weren't?"

"Benny?" The vines loosened slightly. "Benny, as in Benny 'Bones' Barton?"

Pete hesitated. What was the right thing to say? If the bush was Benny's friend, Pete could be in real trouble. However, if the bush didn't like Benny, maybe it would try to help him. "Yes. That's him." He tensed, expecting the bush to violently come down on him.

"I'll tell you what, kid." The restraints unraveled and recoiled into the bush. "I'll give you one more opportunity to treat me with proper respect. Will you take a twig if I offer it to you?"

Pete's spirits lifted. "Yes, yes. Absolutely, I will." He groaned as he rose to his feet. "Honestly, I never meant to offend you in the first place."

"Here you are, kid." The bush flung a three-inch twig at Pete's feet. Pete picked it up and slipped it into his pocket. "I doubt you were the one who was supposed to deal with me originally. Benny knows better than to come around me. I told him the next time I saw him I'd crush him into powder. He's a coward, a liar, and a cheat. You'll learn that soon enough."

"Yes, I've noticed. Thank you so much for the twig!"

"Oh, one more thing. Now that I've helped you, you have to help me."

Pete's stomach dropped. "What?"

"You didn't think I would give you a twig without a price, did you?"

"I thought you said you'd give it to me freely."

"I did, originally. But you put me through a great deal of stress, and these old branches don't do well with stress."

"Okay then, what is it you need?"

"I need you to find Cyril the groundskeeper and tell him I need a thorough grooming. He hasn't been by in ages. Just look at me. I'm a complete mess." He rustled his branches and some fell to the ground.

Pete clenched his jaw and sighed. "Okay." He had precious little time to complete his list, and now he had something new to add to it. Pete looked at the rolling hills that extended for miles around him. The trouble was where was Cyril?

Chapter Eight

Pete trudged along a narrow dirt path cut between two large fields of tombstones. Nervousness still twinged the pit of his stomach. How in the world had he wound up in such a situation? How was it that a regular boring day had turned into being trapped inside an endless graveyard, challenged by a skeleton to a scavenger hunt to prevent the dead from coming back to life?

Ahead in the darkness, quiet, yet steady footsteps grew closer. Pete looked around for a good place to hide. He wasn't quite ready to face any more weird creatures. Who knew what the mood of an average creature would be in this place. Laying low might be his best bet. He jumped off the path, ran for a large tombstone, and ducked behind it.

On the path, a familiar clattering sounded. It was bones clacking together. Rage built inside Pete. It rose from deep down and swept through his entire body like a roaring wildfire. He leapt from behind the tombstone and ran toward the figure emerging from the darkness.

It *was* Benny.

Pete grabbed him by his tattered, grungy collar and forced him to the ground. Benny was much lighter than normal people. He had no flesh, after all.

"You almost got me killed!" He shook Benny's collar. Benny's head rapidly flailed back and forth.

"Stop, stop!" Benny cried.

Despite wanting to punch Benny, Pete let go. "You need to explain yourself, Benny."

"Wow, you could really break somebody's collarbone like that, you know?" Benny got to his feet then picked up his hat, which had fallen during his tumble, and dusted off his tattered jacket and pant legs.

"You cheated! I want my list back."

"I'm sorry, but that can't be done, my good man. I wouldn't dare break the rules of our little competition."

"Excuse me? You already broke the rules. You stole my list!"

Benny laughed. "My dear boy, why would you even attempt to lecture me on rules when you have no idea what they are in the first place?"

"Yeah, and you knew that and took advantage," Pete grumbled under his breath. Benny had a point, but Pete was not about to give him the satisfaction of knowing it. Pete wished he'd had more of an understanding of the rules before the game had started.

"You had your chance to declare a foul earlier when you found you had the wrong list. However, you allowed me to find my first item, and you found your first item too, from what I understand." Benny removed a cracked pocket watch from his jacket, checked the time then calmly placed the watch back into his pocket. "Basically, we have been bonded to our respective lists by those facts. You agreed to continue forth, knowing full well you had been wronged. You set the standard, my dear boy, not I."

Pete's anger deflated. If what Benny said was true, then there was no chance to switch the lists again. Pete was so overwhelmed by the game at the beginning, he had had no way to know what sort of questions to ask regarding specific rules. Benny might be lying, but there was nothing Pete could do about it since Heikle wasn't around to ask.

"You did a very dirty thing, Benny. You must've been a very terrible person when you were alive."

Benny scratched the top of his head. The sound was similar to fingernails across a chalkboard. Pete cringed. "You know, I don't remember. But you're probably right. I can't imagine being any other way."

How could someone forget who they were? Had death made him forget, or had it been so long since he was alive that he had just plain forgotten over time? Either way, it was pitiful. Nobody, not even Benny, deserved to forget how great life could be.

"Well," said Benny, "if you're finished throwing people to the ground, I suppose I'll continue with *my* list. May the best chap win! Of course, you have no chance whatsoever of winning, but good luck anyway!" Benny plunked his hat onto his head and continued down the path.

"Hey, Benny!"

Benny stopped and turned. "Yes?"

"How many items have you found on your list so far?" Pete asked. How far behind Benny was he?

"That's a major breach of etiquette, young man. But what the heck, I'm feeling charitable. Since this was your list to begin with, I suppose it won't hurt."

Benny reached into his coat pocket then into the hip pocket of his pants. Then the rear pocket. He removed his bowler hat and looked in the lining. He grew more frantic with every pocket he found empty. "Oh, dear. It seems I've dropped it somewhere."

Pete crumbled Benny's list tighter and tighter in his hand. He wanted so much to tear it into tiny pieces and throw them into Benny's face.

But cheating was the wrong way to go about winning. Besides, he still didn't know the rules. If he destroyed or hid the list, he might have to suffer a penalty. He dropped the paper to the ground then kicked it off the dirt path. "Oh, here it is, Benny. You must've dropped it when you fell earlier."

Benny stormed over, picked up the list and smoothed the wrinkles from it. "You mean when you *tackled* me?" Benny sneered, or at least Pete imagined he did. "There is a long way to go before this little game is over. Things get more and more dangerous as we go. I'd hate to see something ... ghastly happen to you."

Was that a threat? And if "things get more and more dangerous," Pete would be lucky to make it out alive.

"Well then, I hope I can rely on your help if I find myself in some serious trouble." Though he probably shouldn't accept any help from Benny. But even with all the tricks, Benny had to have limits to his meanness.

Benny folded his list and slid it into his coat pocket. "Perhaps. You never know. If I'm close by, I suppose I could spare a few moments of my time, if you are indeed in need of serious help. Let's just hope you don't catch Gaug in a foul mood. If you cross him, there is nothing I can do to save you." Benny gave a curt bow and tipped his bowler hat. He strolled away on the dirt path and disappeared into the darkness.

Chapter Nine

Pete stopped at a fork in the road. Massive, moss-covered trees lined both paths, creating dark tunnels he was hesitant to enter. There was no telling how long he had been walking. It felt like forever. His legs aching, he sat on a large rock directly across from a mangy-looking scarecrow propped against a tree.

He glanced at his list, which seemed to grow longer by the minute then shoved it into his pocket. He wished he had never set foot in the graveyard. He should've listened to Papaw.

"You sure look awful agitated. You must be busy thinking, huh?"

Pete jumped at the voice that shattered the silence of the graveyard.

"Oh, I guess I scared you. I'm good at that, you know. I scare crows, after all." The voice chuckled.

A talking scarecrow? Well, why not, there was a man-eating bush and a living skeleton. There might as well be a talking scarecrow too.

"You sure don't talk much, do ya? What's wrong with you anyway?"

"There's nothing wrong with me. You just caught me by surprise. That's all."

"Oh, he does talk!"

"Sure, I can talk. You're the one that shouldn't be able to."

"Excuse me?" The scarecrow's canvas face wrinkled, making his eyes angry. "Judging by your age, I've been talking longer than you've been breathing!"

"I'm sorry. I didn't mean to insult you. It's just everything here is different from what I'm used to." Pete shook his head. Everyone he'd met had been easily aggravated.

"Aw, that's okay." The scarecrow's face smoothed again. "It's just nice to get a chance to talk to somebody every once in a while. My name is Dusty. They propped me way out here in the middle of nowhere. Don't ask me why. No crows ever come this way. A few vultures and buzzards, but no crows. So, what brings you here?"

Pete pulled the list from his pocket. "This. I'm on a scavenger hunt. I'm lost and don't have the slightest idea where any of this stuff is." Pete glanced at the second item on the list. "Hey, wait! You're name is Dusty? You're the second entry on the list!"

"Me? Why the devil would you need to collect me? Somebody must have a cruel sense of humor. Does it hurt to be collected? I don't recall ever being collected before."

"Well, I don't really need *all* of you. I just need a straw from your head. That's all."

"That's all? Are you serious? How do you suppose I'll think without it? Maybe I give you the wrong straw and my arms stop working. Or maybe if I grab one, all my precious memories get wiped away forever? How about I take a straw from *your* head?"

Pete imagined pulling something out of himself simply because someone had asked him to. He couldn't even imagine doing it. Pete swallowed hard. He'd had no idea how big the request was when he made it.

"Gee whiz, kid. You sure don't have respect for your fellow man, do you?" Dusty crossed his arms, but one of his hands fell off. "Now look! You've got me so upset that I'm going to pieces. This is just great!"

"Look, I'm sorry, Dusty. Maybe there's some other way."

"Some other way to mutilate me, you mean? Sure, why don't you get a pitchfork or a rake and bash my head in? That should do it! There will be plenty of straws then. You can take whichever one you want."

"I said I'm sorry. But it's the second item on my list. I really need one. Otherwise, I'll never go home. If I lose, my world will be horribly different."

"Why should I care? I rarely get any visitors. Only 'Bones' Barton comes to see me. He's my only friend in the world."

Why would Benny's friend be on what was supposed to be his list? Wouldn't Dusty have helped him out willingly? Then again, maybe whoever created the lists would've thought even Benny wouldn't stoop so low as to hurt a friend without some hesitation.

"That's even more incentive for you to help me! If I lose this scavenger hunt, Benny will go to my world and you'll never see him again. You'll be all alone here. Everybody from your world will go to mine!"

"Who said that?"

"Benny did!"

Dusty's shoulders slouched. "So he'd up and leave, just like that? I thought he said we were pals."

"I don't know what he told you, but he told me he was going to win, no matter what. So if you don't help me, he will win and you'll be all alone forever, because even when people die, they won't come here anymore."

Dusty slowly nodded. "Okay. I'll help you. But you have to promise you won't lose the straw I pull. I'm giving up a lot by doing this, you know?"

"I know, Dusty, but I really need to win. Not just for me, but for you too, of course!"

Dusty stared. His eyes were two black holes in a canvas head, but they conveyed a message all the same—a message of fear.

"Okay then. Let's see here." He raised one arm and lowered it again. It was the arm without a hand. He reached up with his good arm and probed through a loose seam in his canvas head.

Pete nervously watched. Hopefully, it wouldn't be painful. The scarecrow was sacrificing a lot just so he could still have the occasional company of his supposed friend, the liar and cheater Benny "Bones" Barton.

Dusty's left eye twitched and his cheek flinched. He screamed.

Pete's stomach clinched and he felt like crying.

Dusty suddenly stopped screaming and started laughing. "You should've seen your face!"

Pete was both relieved and angry. How could someone make a sick joke in such a tense situation? Could he even trust Dusty?

"Okay, okay. I'll do it for real this time." Dusty dug his fingers further into his canvas skin and probed.

Finally, he pulled out a long, slender, golden straw. "How did that get in there?"

Pete chuckled.

"Ew, gross!" Dusty dropped the straw to the ground. "You know, young man, if you put a little sugar on corn, it gets down right disgusting."

"What?"

"I said, if you catch a bear by its tail, you had better get dressed one leg at a time because the trees will be rotten."

Dusty must have pulled a straw he shouldn't have. Pete felt terrible, but he desperately needed that straw. "Dusty, do you know where Melvin's Pond is? I really need to get there. I've spent too much time here already."

"Sure, Mervin's Pond. You just take that fork in the road."

"I said, Melvin's Pond. And take which direction in the fork?"

"You've got it! Boy you're as sharp as apple butter in a snow storm."

It was useless. Dusty couldn't form a rational thought. Pete was off to find the next destination by himself, yet again.

Chapter Ten

Pete studied the fork in the path, looking down one direction and then the other. Dusty had said to "take the fork," but which one? Both were dark and misty. Both were lined with trees covered with greasy moss.

Pete was worried. Dusty's thoughts had been bouncing off the inside of his skull like a marble in a spray paint can. It might have been by complete coincidence that he even mentioned the fork. Who knew where the wrong path would lead.

Time is wasting. Pete went with the left path. Desperately hoping he was heading in the right direction, he looked for signs that would tip him off as to what was ahead.

Several brown leaves skittered across the path as a breeze picked up. He shivered then rubbed his upper arms. Somehow, in the hullabaloo, he had failed to realize it was quite chilly in the graveyard. The air grew colder the further he walked, reminding Pete of the times he used to go fishing with his dad at Taylorsville Lake. They would leave the house before the sun even came up, and it would be crisp and cool out. Once they got to the lake, the air would have even more of a bite to it.

Perhaps Melvin's Pond is up ahead! Pete increased his pace. As the air grew colder with each step, his confidence grew. A thin mist covered the ground. The colder he got, the more the mist thickened. Eventually, Pete lost sight of his feet. It was as if he was running on his knees on top of the mist.

He stopped when the ground suddenly softened. It was a slimy, muddy mess, and the smell was terrible, like the dumpster full of rotten fish behind Jake's All-You-Can-Eat Seafood. *I must be standing on the pond bank.* All he needed to find was a single strand of seaweed, and then he could go on to his next item.

He scanned the frothy mist that spread over the pond like a large baseball field made of cotton. As far as he could see, there was a floor of mist until the shadowy darkness swallowed it up. There were no breaks, and there was no guarantee that there was a pond at all. It could be a never-ending cavernous hole. Pete edged back and sighed deeply. The only way to find out what was beyond the mud was to take a step forward.

The longer I spend thinking about it, the closer Benny could be to finishing up his list. Pete sloshed back into the mud and carefully reached through the mist. His fingertips touched something cool. Water! As quickly as he could manage without losing his balance, he dipped his arm deep into the water and wrapped his fingers around a grimy strand. Seaweed? His heart fluttered. He hated not being able to see what he was grabbing.

He tugged at the strand, but it didn't come loose. He bent down and dug his heels in so he could get better leverage. Then he pulled harder. The strand shifted, as if to pull free from his hand, but just barely. Perhaps it wasn't seaweed at all. Maybe he had grabbed something else. But what?

The burning, nervous feeling in his stomach returned. He wasn't pulling at seaweed at all. It felt more like strands of hair. Someone with grimy, slimy hair was at the bottom of the pond.

Pete let go and retreated as something broke the surface of the water. Whoever, or whatever, it was, was rising.

Through the mist, the top of someone's head broke. It was a man. His hair was covered with mossy grime. His face was puffy and wrinkled. He had a long, stringy mustache that draped down his chin.

Pete had probably grabbed the man's mustache. He discreetly wiped his fingers on his blue jeans.

"Who are you?" The puffy man spoke in a deep and gravelly voice with a slight gurgle to it. "Why do you dare trespass on my property? Can you not read? There are plenty of signs posted along the way!"

Pete's entire body shook. "I-I'm s-s-sorry. I never saw any signs. Ar-are you Mr. Melvin? Is this your pond?"

"Melvin? I hate Melvin!" roared the man. "My name is Mervin! If you are a friend of Melvin, then you are no friend of mine, and I promise you this will be the last pond you ever see!" Mervin stood tall. He had to be at least seven feet in height. He trudged toward Pete.

Pete looked around for something to defend himself with, but there was nothing around except tombstones too large and heavy to lift. "Look, Mr. Melv—"

"What?" Mervin roared.

"I mean, Mr. Mervin. Look, Mr. Mervin, I'm lost. I had no idea this was your pond. There were no signs, I swear! I don't even know Mr. Melvin! To tell you the truth, I don't even want to be here. I just want to go home!"

"Well, young man, you should have considered that before you trespassed on my property. Do you know how long it takes for me to culture a proper mud bank? Do you realize you just cost me three months of hard work?" Mervin towered over Pete.

Pete wouldn't be able to outrun Mervin. The man was too big to get away from. But Pete had no other option.

Pete turned. Before he could move an inch, two powerful hands clutched his arms.

Chapter Eleven

The dirt path shrunk away as Pete was lifted off the ground. He kicked his legs, but it was no use. There was no escaping Mervin's giant, shriveled fingers.

"You dared to trespass? You should never trespass on someone's property or take what is not yours!" Mervin held Pete high above his head. "Some people just have to learn the hard way."

"Wait!" A faint, yet familiar voice called from the dirt path below.

Pete saw a bleach-white tiny figure in a pin-striped suit and a bowler hat. Benny!

"Wait, Mervin! Wait!" Benny called through his boney hands he'd cupped around his mouth.

"What do you want, Bones? I'm going to teach this young man a lesson. I'll be with you in a moment. On second thought, can you come back later? This may take a while."

"No, that's why I'm here. It's not his fault he came here. He's a bit slow in the head. You know, too many brains and not enough good sense."

"Bones, this does not concern you!"

"Ah, but it does. He's my newest challenger."

Mervin grumbled, "You'll owe me, Bones."

"Indeed I will. I'll find the vilest pond possible for you on the other side."

Mervin dropped Pete on the ground. Pete landed hard on his shoulder. He met Mervin's glare. Mervin's jaw muscles rippled as if he still wanted to punish Pete but chose instead to grind his teeth together to contain his rage.

"Boy," said Mervin, "If I ever catch you near my pond again, not even Bones will be able to save you. Do you understand me?"

Pete scrambled to his feet. "Yes, sir. I'll never come this way again. I promise!" He meant it. Had he known this was not Melvin's Pond, he would never have entered.

"Now, get out of my sight. The both of you!" Mervin roared.

"Yeah, yeah. We're on our way," Benny said. "Come on, Pete, let's get you out of here."

Pete and Benny walked in silence for some distance. Pete rubbed his throbbing shoulder. The disgusting smell of Mervin's pond clung to his clothes. Eventually the silence became too much and he asked, "So why did you come and save me?"

Benny shrugged. "I don't know. I guess I felt guilty. I also knew what might happen if you wound up at the wrong pond. You should've gone right at the fork, you know."

"I figured out that much, Benny. I just wish there had been signs. Mervin said there are, but I didn't see any."

Benny chuckled nervously. "Yeah, that's why I felt a little guilty. There actually were signs. When you saw me on the path earlier, I'd just finished removing them."

"You what?"

"Hey, I already said I felt guilty! What, do you want my head on a platter, too? I suppose if you bring me a platter, I can oblige. I don't think you'd want it, though. I do talk a lot."

"Why would you do that, Benny? You almost got me killed again! One of these little shortcuts of yours is going to get me into a situation I can't get out of. Then what? I doubt you'll feel guilty when I'm dead. In fact, I'd say you'd be happy. That way you could play tricks on me day in and day out!"

"You know, that's not a bad idea," Benny said, stroking his jaw.

Pete stopped and stared wide-eyed at Benny. Was Benny really thinking of killing him? He was a trickster, a liar, and a cheat, but was he a murderer?

Benny laughed. "I'm just pulling your leg. Come on, Pete. You need to lighten up a bit."

Pete's heart rate was still elevated. Had Benny only been joking? Instead of pressing him on the subject, Pete asked, "So, how many items have you found so far?"

"Oh, no you don't. I was willing enough to tell you earlier, before you decided to hide and crumple my list. That's right. Don't think I don't know how it wound up on the ground. Now, I'll just let the suspense eat you up."

"Aw, come on. I bet you don't even have the first thing. You just made that up earlier."

"Do too! I'm not going to fall for your childish reverse-psychology tricks either, Pete. Seriously, I was using them before Orville was even born."

"So, how was my papaw? I mean, was he good at the scavenger hunt?"

"Shoot, are you kidding me? I threw every trick in the book at him, but he was always a step ahead. That guy is savvy, certainly more so than you. No offense. Heck, there were a couple times he even tricked *me*. One of those little tricks cost me the game."

"Oh really?"

"Yep. I tried to steal one of the items he had collected, a shoelace from Iggy Zelman's sneaker. Well, he planned ahead. He switched his own shoelace with the one he took from Iggy. I beat him to the finish, but I lost since I didn't have the right items from the list. That's why they made it so I couldn't steal anything this time. It's a good thing, too. But don't think I'd fall for that trick twice. I'd take both of your shoes and the shoestring, too!"

Pete thought about the little practical jokes Papaw had played earlier. His papaw was full of life and a kid at heart. Pete hoped to get to know him better.

But first thing was first, he had to finish his list before Benny completed his. But by Benny's own admission, he would cheat to win. Pete had to think of a way to trick Benny the way his papaw had. After another few yards along the path, Benny and Pete reached the fork.

"Well, I suppose this is good-bye," said Benny. "Good luck and stay out of trouble. I doubt I'll be helping you again. I have a list to get to, you know." Benny turned to leave but stopped. "Oh, one last thing. This is for you." Benny handed Pete a slimy strand of seaweed. "It's from Melvin's Pond. It's the least I could do. He owed me a favor, and he's twice as mean and nasty as Mervin." Benny chuckled.

Pete shivered with excitement. Benny had done him a great kindness. Maybe he had really felt guilty after all.

Pete was ready to get started again. He had a lot of planning to do. Most of all, he had to think of a way to trick Benny. The thought made him feel guilty, but Benny had every advantage in the game, and it was time to turn the tables. "Good luck to you too, Benny. Thanks for the seaweed. If you don't somehow get me killed, I'll see you later, after *I've* won the game."

Benny laughed and tipped his hat. "That, my good man, will not happen." He whistled a tune as he strolled away.

Chapter Twelve

Pete took out the list. There were only three things left, not counting that he had to find Cyril the groundskeeper. The next item was, "Hair from a pig's tail from Hilda's Hut."

He followed the path. A blurry patch of clouds spread and parted to allow the full moon to light everything with an eerie silver glow.

A strange noise caught his attention. It sounded like a cat crying in pain, or some sort of siren blaring in the distance. He strained his ears and tried to locate it. The closer he got, the louder it grew. It was coming from somewhere among the graves off the path and into the darkness.

Pete stood at the path's edge, hesitant to continue into the jungle of tombstones and crypts. If he were to get lost in that maze, he might never find his way out.

Just before he stepped off the trail, he noticed the noise was growing louder. The source was coming nearer. The more he listened, the more the noise resembled crude music. It was almost as if someone was humming or singing some terrible song. How could anyone produce such a horrible sound?

Twenty or so feet away, twigs snapped. It was a woman singing, terribly.

Pete held his ground. Who was she? Perhaps she knew who Hilda was. Perhaps she could help him find the next item on the list. Then he'd be more than halfway finished.

The woman was horribly ugly. She was very short, and very dumpy. She wore a ragged gray dress and a dirty white apron with large pockets filled with strange-looking plants. Her long, wiry hair was covered with brambles. Warts covered her bulbous nose. As she sang her bizarre, nonsensical song, she carried a large burlap sack over her shoulder.

"Hello?" Pete called.

"Oh my word!" shrieked the old woman. She dropped her bag, and it fell open and spilled its contents, which appeared to be bones. "Who are you, you mongrel? And how dare you sneak up on a poor old woman." She placed her hand over her chest.

"I'm sorry. I didn't mean to scare you. I was just hoping you could help me. I need to find someone named Hilda."

She tilted her head and narrowed her eyes. "What do you know about her, and why do you need to find her?"

"Well, I have this list. It's part of a scavenger hunt. I need the hair of a pig's tail from Hilda's Hut. I was thinking you might know where I can find her."

"I suppose I do. I've known her all my life. In fact, she's me." She cackled, exposing several crooked brown and blackened teeth in yellowed gums. "Come. Follow me. I'll lead the way to my hut. It's no trouble at all. Just let me get my things."

Hilda pushed the bones back into the burlap bag then cinched it shut. She grunted a bit as she slung the bag over her shoulder. Afterward, she seemed to have no problem under the bag's weight as she led Pete through a very dark portion of the graveyard.

"So, is it far? I still have a couple more things to get."

"No, no. You just hang with me. We're almost there. If it's a pig you want, it's a pig you'll get," Hilda said with a wink.

Soon enough they made it to a shabby hut made of mud and straw. It smelled like damp, musty grass. "Here we are," she said, "home, sweet home."

Pete was excited. Only two more items left after the pig's hair. He hoped the rest of the list was as easy to come by as the pig's hair.

"You look famished! Let me cook you up something. It won't take but a moment."

"No, thanks. I'm fine. The quicker I finish the scavenger hunt, the better. I appreciate the offer, though."

Hilda looked disappointed, almost hurt. "Well, let me fix you some tea then. It won't take any time at all, and I won't take no for an answer!" She flashed Pete her disgusting, crooked smile.

A pot of tea shouldn't take but a few minutes, and she's been nothing but helpful so far. "Okay, fine. I'm not a big fan of tea, but I'll have some if you want some."

"Splendid! I'll boil the water right away." Hilda threw open grassy cabinet doors and rattled the pots, metallic goblets, and cups around. A rat scurried past her foot, possibly fleeing from the frenzied noise. "You come back here, Patrick!" She grabbed a straw broom, corralled the rat then placed it into a wooden box on the counter. "Silly rat is always running away."

Pete scanned the hut while Hilda cranked water from a hand pump and lit a flame on the stovetop. The ceiling was nothing more than bundles of tall grass laid over a framework of crooked tree branches. The walls, caked with dried mud, seemed a bit sturdier. Several strands of yellowed grass protruded here and there. He was quite impressed with the cozy hut.

"It won't be but another moment or two! You just sit tight!" Hilda called over the clamoring of the cast-iron cookware.

Pete galloped his fingers on the tabletop. The lack of conversation became slightly uncomfortable. He searched for something to talk about and remembered the burlap bag Hilda had been carrying. Why would she need a bag of bones? Would it be an okay subject to talk about? "What was in that bag?" He bit his lip, scared he may have crossed a line, wishing he could take back the words.

Hilda darted a hard glare at Pete. Her eyes were like two fiery dots in the center of her lumpy face. "My business is my own, so stay out of it!"

Pete fumbled for something to say. "I-I'm sorry. I was just curious. I was trying to make conversation."

Her face softened. "Yes, yes, I understand. You are an inquisitive one, aren't you? Well, if you must know, they were, uh, stolen from my, uh, personal graveyard. Yes, vandals live amongst us, you know."

By her tone, she was either lying or only telling half of the truth, but he didn't press her. He wasn't sure how fast she could go from nervous to angry, so he just nodded.

She turned with a cup of steaming liquid. "Now, here you go. You drink this up. It will warm you." Hilda pulled a pig's tail from her apron pocket and plucked a single hair from it. She slid it into Pete's shirt pocket. "I think this is what you asked me for, right?"

"Yes, ma'am. Thank you very much. You have been very helpful." Pete smelled the tea. It had a strange scent to it. He brought it closer to his lips.

Hilda's eyes widened. She rubbed her hands together.

Pete didn't like how she looked at him. "Where's your cup, Hilda?"

"Oh, uh, I only had enough to make one cup!"

It was strange she was so willing to be helpful for nothing in return. She was just a little *too* eager to be nice. "Well, I feel bad. I don't want to drink your last cup of tea."

"Nonsense, you drink it. Drink it up, now!" She was breathing heavily, and her hands moved frantically, nervously tugging at one another.

Pete intentionally fumbled and dropped the metal cup on the table. "Oops!" Tea spilled onto the tabletop.

"No!" shrieked Hilda. "You little fool. How dare you!"

The table began to sprout fur. A long, rat-like tail grew from the table's edge.

"I will get you for that!" she screeched. She lunged toward Pete.

There was nowhere for him to go. His chair was lodged between the table and the mud wall. Perhaps if he crawled under the table, he could escape. But before he could slide from his chair, two powerful, hairy arms busted through the wall behind him, wrapped around him, and squeezed tight, forcing the air out of him.

And Hilda was just inches away.

Chapter Thirteen

The arms clamped tighter around Pete's chest. He wasn't sure if it was the wall or his ribcage cracking and crumbling until large clumps of dried mud fell over his head. Hilda jumped back just as the roof caved in.

The arms loosened. Pete stared at the cloud-covered sky, trying to catch his breath.

"You wrecked my hut, Cyril!" Hilda screeched. "How dare you tear down my house."

"Shut up, hag," a voice boomed.

"You'll mind your tongue if you don't want it in one of my stews!"

Pete finally sat up and saw a massive hunch-backed figure. His gray shirt draped loosely around his shoulders and hung down to brown pants held up with a strand of rope.

"Ah!" Cyril dismissed Hilda with a wave of his arm. "I'm done with you, hag. Stop bothering people, or else you will answer to me."

"You came just in time! She was going to kill me!" Pete said to Cyril.

"No kidding! Don't you know any better than to run around with witches? She could've turned you into a rat or a toad, or even something worse. Where do you think she got all those bones? She sure didn't dig them up!" Cyril helped Pete to his feet and they moved away from the crumbling hut.

Pete felt nauseous again. He'd come very close to being turned into a rat. Then he'd come even closer to being killed at the hands of a real-life witch. He'd had his fill of adventure for one night.

As if reading his mind, Cyril added, "You won't have to worry about her anymore. She'll be working on her shack for weeks before it's fixed again."

Pete sighed. "I really just want to get this list finished and go home. This is all too much. I can't imagine what would happen if Benny actually won. I can't live with the people from this place for the rest of my life." He looked at Cyril's sad, crooked face. "No offense, Cyril. You seem to be nice. You certainly saved my life, but I'm used to living in the sun and not having to worry about being killed at every turn."

Cyril's face lightened. "Ah, I'm sure you'll beat Benny. Everyone else sure does."

"What do you mean, 'everyone else'? He's done this more than twice?"

"Oh yeah. He's been put in charge of merging our world with yours. I have to say I'm not a big fan of the idea. I like this place just as it is really, but the powers that be want it done, so I guess it will be done eventually."

"So why doesn't he just do it then? Why does he challenge us to games?"

"Oh, that's his personality. He loves to play games, and every now and then, one of you catches him at just the right time. But I'd say the powers that be are getting rather tired of all his failures. This may be his last chance. Since he almost won it last time, I don't doubt he'll do anything to win this time around."

"Well, I'm really glad you found me. You were actually next up on my list."

"Really? Is that a fact? How may I be of service?"

"So far I've collected a twig from the nearest bush, which by the way, he asked for me to get you to stop by so you can groom him; a straw from Dusty's head; a strand of seaweed from Melvin's Pond; and a hair from a pig's tail from Hilda's Hut. Now I need a blue-flamed lantern from your shanty."

"Well, you've been very busy, huh? May I see the items?"

Pete hesitated. How trustworthy was Cyril?

"I can see you're nervous, as you should be. But I can be trusted. Though since hardly anyone else around here can be, you don't have to show them to me if you'd rather not."

Pete felt a little more comforted by Cyril's sincerity. He had asked pleasantly and his eyes looked kind enough, despite his looks. *Besides, he rescued me from Hilda. I owe him at least a little trust.*

"Okay, I guess I can trust you." He pulled the items from his pockets and showed them one at a time.

"Where did you say you got that seaweed?"

"From Melvin's Pond. Why?"

"That seaweed is not from Melvin's Pond. I know everything there is to know about the grounds of this graveyard. That strand is definitely from Mervin's Pond, not Melvin's."

Pete slapped his hand to his forehead. "I should've known better! Now I have to go all the way back there to get another one!"

"Let me guess. Bones offered you a little help?"

"Yes. He almost got me killed then gave me this as a truce."

Cyril laughed. "Don't worry. I have some back at my shanty, and I will gladly share it with you. Melvin is a good friend of mine. I even have an extra blue-flamed lantern."

"Thank you so much! I wish there was something I could do to repay you. I really appreciate it!"

"There is."

Pete hesitated, tension slowly building in anticipation of what Cyril would say. Almost every other deal so far had come at a high price. What would Cyril ask for? With no other choice, he asked. "Okay, what is it?"

Cyril smiled. "You can beat that good-for-nothing skeleton and keep our worlds separated. I really don't think the sun would be good for my delicate complexion."

Pete and Cyril laughed as they entered the shanty. "Well, this is my place. It's no paradise, but it's cozy, and it's home." It was a simple home, more like a large shed. The walls and roof were nothing more than old gray, splintered wood. All of Cyril's tools hung from nails driven into the walls. A single lantern with a blazing blue flame provided light.

Cyril opened a large wooden chest in the corner. He flung spades, rakes, scythes and hammers from it. Finally, he stood upright with a reddened face. "Here it is! As promised, one genuine, blue-flamed lantern just for you. Ah! I almost forgot!" Cyril walked over to the kitchen, which was nothing more than a large skillet resting over a blackened hearth. He opened another smaller chest and rummaged around until he pulled a strand of gray seaweed from it. "Here you go! See, this is much more firm and the coloring is much, much nicer than those nasty strands Mervin has."

"I suppose so," Pete said with a smile.

"Now off with you! You go beat that suit full of bones! Don't let him pull the wool over your eyes again!"

Again, they shared a laugh, but it was cut short when the door burst open.

Chapter Fourteen

There in the doorway stood Benny. He held out his list. "Okay, hunchback, I need a spade!"

"Must you always break the door open? I'm getting tired of fixing it," groaned Cyril. "All you have to do is knock. I'll open it for you in no time."

"Yeah, whatever. So where is it? If it's on the list, it must be here. Fork it over, lumpy." Benny looked at Pete. "Oh wow, look who's here! How's your list coming along? Two things left? Three?"

"You won't tell me, so I won't tell you!" snapped Pete. He was still angry about Benny intentionally giving him the wrong seaweed. Then again, he was almost as mad at himself for falling for it. He and Benny had just had a conversation about how bad of a cheater Benny was before the skeleton gave him the strand.

"Okay, okay, calm yourself." Benny squeezed into a seat at the table beside where Pete stood. "Hey, fatso! I've asked you twice now. Where's the spade?"

"There is no spade. My last one broke a few days ago. I need to get a new one soon." Pete looked over at Cyril, who was putting tools back into their chest. Cyril made sure Benny could not see the small spades he had tossed aside earlier by blocking Benny's view with his wide body.

"You're joking? Yes, I'm a skeleton, but mind you, I was born without a funny bone, fat man! You are supposed to be a groundskeeper. What kind of miserable excuse of a groundskeeper goes without a spade? You had better find one, and quick."

"Why do you have to be so mean?" asked Pete. "Cyril has been nothing but nice to me since I've met him. That's way more than I can say for you."

"That's the only way to talk to Cyril, you know. Between you and me," said Benny. He cupped his hands around his mouth. "he's a little slow."

"Okay, Bones. Coming right up," said Cyril.

Barely able to wedge between the table and the wall, Cyril squeezed into a chair across from Benny. He held a shabby deck of cards, dingy and gray with age. The corners were split and the edges were frayed. "These are my favorite playing cards. Of course, every deck of cards has thirteen hearts, thirteen clubs, thirteen diamonds, and—"

"And thirteen spades. Yes, yes, hand them over," Benny said.

"What's the hurry, Benny? You aren't nervous about the game, are you? Surely you haven't heard the rumors you might be replaced if you fail again. I wouldn't believe them anyway if I were you." Cyril winked at Pete. "So anyway, as I was saying—"

"You've said enough already! I need the spade! The spade! Now!" Benny banged his bony fist on the table.

"Okay, Benny. I'll give you the spade. In fact, I'll give all of them to you." Cyril handed Benny the deck of cards.

Benny leapt from the chair and made for the door.

"Oh, Bones. Just one more thing before you go."

"Yes, what is it?"

"I challenge you to a game of poker. This game will be a hard one, though. The cards change at random every few minutes or so. You may be holding a king of hearts, and then a moment later, it will be a seven of clubs or maybe a nine of diamonds. You can never tell what your hand will look like. You may have a winner one moment and a bust the next. That's the fun of it. That is, of course, unless you aren't up to it."

Benny slid to a stop in the doorway. He peeked over his shoulder at Pete then rushed back to his chair. "Okay, okay, but hurry!"

Pete remembered what Cyril had told him, *Benny loves games*. It was almost more like an addiction from Benny's frantic behavior.

"Pete, don't you have somewhere you need to be?" Cyril smiled at Pete.

Pete smiled and silently mouthed, "thank you."

Cyril gave a nod.

"Come on! Deal the cards already!" yelled Benny. He stood up nervously and shifted from foot to foot before sitting back down.

Pete walked toward the door.

"Take your time, kid. Don't forget, Gaug is a rather surly fellow. In fact, I think he's been in a bit of a bad mood here lately. I may have accidentally let it slip you had to swing by there and borrow something of his. He was most displeased."

For the second time, Pete swore he saw a smile on Benny's face, even though he was nothing more than bone. "Thanks a lot, Benny."

"You have to go to Gaug's place?" Cyril asked. His face turned even whiter than it already was. "What on earth do you need to get from there?"

"A bone from his scrap pile."

Benny laughed. He laughed so hard the hat on his head vibrated.

"Are you sure?" asked Cyril.

"That's what it says on my list. See: 'a bone from Gaug's scrap pile' right here." Pete held it to where Cyril could read it.

"Oh my." Cyril's face turned a light shade of green.

Pete felt a wave of dread wash over him. "Why does everyone act like that? Is Gaug really that bad? I mean, who is Gaug, anyway?"

Cyril eased back in his chair and fanned himself with his cards. Benny's shoulders continued to shake and rattle with laughter.

"Gaug is a ghoul," said Cyril. "He goes around and digs up freshly-buried bodies, so he can eat them. He sucks the meat right off the bones. Then those bones are added to his collection, a shrine he's dedicated to himself, you could say. Nobody around here messes with Gaug, and if I were you, I would be extremely careful. I would just grab what you need, pray he is nowhere in sight, and run. If he gets a hold of you, no one can save you."

"So why is Benny laughing like that?"

Benny shook his head. "I'm sorry. I really shouldn't laugh. It is actually quite terrible." Another wave of laughter drowned out the rest of his words. His head thunked onto the table, and he dropped his cards.

He was hysterical with laughter. "That's okay, Benny. I can still get in and out of there in no time. I'm going to win, and you'll be stuck here forever. Then we'll see whose laughing."

"Sure we will, sport. You go get that bone now." Benny threw his head back, laughed again, and repeatedly banged his fist on the table.

"Just keep laughing. I don't care. I'm out of here. Oh, and it's my last stop, Benny."

Benny poked his head up again and stopped laughing.

"That's right. It's the last item on the list. Oh, and I know you gave me a bogus strand of seaweed. Nice try, jerk. I've got the real thing now, so you haven't tricked me out of winning yet. Have fun losing the scavenger hunt!"

"Hurry this game up, ugly!" Benny yelled at Cyril. He couldn't sit still. He rocked back and forth in his chair, repeatedly removing and replacing his hat.

Pete smiled, knowing Benny was near panicked because he hadn't outsmarted Pete. Feeling slightly better, Pete left him there. *Let Benny feel miserable.* He deserved it.

Now Pete was on to the biggest challenge. He didn't look forward to meeting Gaug, who knew he was coming thanks to Benny. There was no telling what kind of danger awaited him at the end of the dirt path.

Chapter Fifteen

As Pete drew closer to Gaug's den, his heart rate accelerated. The dirt path seemed darker and the trees seemed more sinister. The air smelled absolutely foul. It was no wonder most everything in the graveyard avoided Gaug's den.

What did a ghoul look like? He had heard of them in books but couldn't imagine how they appeared in real life, assuming this graveyard scavenger hunt wasn't a nightmare.

He came to the bottom of a steep hill. Just in case Gaug was actually expecting him, Pete decided get off the path. Thanks to Benny, Gaug was probably fuming in rage over the thought of Pete taking one of his prized bones. Pete imagined running into the ghoul on the path just outside his den and shuddered.

He tiptoed behind one of the dark, gnarled trees and stepped on a fallen branch. Against the silence of Gaug's den, the sound of the branch's snap was nearly deafening. Pete panicked and hunkered down behind the tree, hiding in its shadow.

An intense growl came from a large cave in the neighboring hillside twenty feet away. A cloud of dust bellowed out in front of the large presence that stormed to the cave's edge. The silhouette against the dimly lit cave was massive. It had to be twelve feet in height. The creature had short legs but massive and powerful-looking arms.

Pete's heart raced. How in the world was he to get a bone and get away without Gaug noticing?

The ghoul growled again then disappeared into the cave. Pete was frozen to the tree. He had to come up with a plan. There had to be a way to get passed Gaug. How would Benny do it? He scanned the area. There looked to be only one entrance and exit. Things had just got harder.

He leaned back against the tree. How could he lure Gaug from his cave? Set a fire? That was too cruel. Create a noisy diversion? With what? And how long would that last? Not long, most likely.

A steady stream of foul-smelling, hot air blew across Pete's back. He turned and saw a knee covered with brown hair. His gaze followed the knee upward to dirty tan, tattered shorts. Those led to a grimy, stained white shirt, which led to a massive head. That head had a huge mouth with long, yellow and brown teeth jutting out in all directions and two, small, yellow eyes. Knobby, brown warts covered the face. There was nothing and nobody so ugly.

"Who are you?" the monstrous creature boomed.

Pete went limp like a dishrag. He was too scared to run, too intimidated to speak, and too surprised to think.

"I said, who are you?" the creature repeated angrily. His beady eyes were like two tiny flames of rage.

"I, uh, I-" Pete struggled to speak. He was dumbfounded by the giant who stood before him. Despite all he'd seen in the graveyard, Gaug was the most monstrous and intimidating.

"Answer me!"

"My name it Pete Davidson," he finally squeaked out.

"Bones told me about you! You came here to steal my trophies!"

"No, sir. I just need to borrow one bone. You can have it back as soon as I'm done with it."

"What do you mean, 'when you're done with it'? Why do you assume I would let you steal my belongings in the first place?" The monster shook with anger.

"I didn't assume anything. I just have this list I have to complete. That's all."

"Then why are you sneaking up on my home? How would you feel if I snuck up on your home and threatened to steal your things?"

Pete saw a glimmer of hope. Gaug seemed willing to talk as opposed to just smashing him into the ground. "If I had known you were as reasonable as you are, I would've just asked you in the first place."

"But you didn't, did you? Thank goodness Bones let me know you were on the way. I usually can't trust him at all. It looks as if, for once, he told me something truthful." The monster clinched his massive, clawed hands into fists. "I'm not sure what it is that has kept me from tearing you apart so far, but my patience is wearing thin. You had better come up with a good explanation, or else your bones will be the newest pieces in my collection!"

Pete's mind raced. What could be said that would save him from Gaug? Then it hit him. "Benny told you that so he could win the game we're playing. He wants to merge your world with mine. He wants to make it to where you have to live in the world of the living."

"Do what?" Gaug roared.

"Yep. He wants to live where the sun shines all day long and the night only comes for a few hours. There are lots of graveyards there, but they are small and far apart from each other. You'd have to walk for miles just to find one."

"You're lying!"

"Nope. You mean he didn't tell you? He didn't tell you why he came to you?" Pete remembered what he was originally supposed to ask from Gaug. Fresh flies. "He didn't ask for fresh flies?"

"Yes, yes, he did. I gave him a jar full."

"That put him one step closer to living in the sunlight with flowers and butterflies and furry little kittens."

Gaug's dark green skin paled. He placed a hand on his forehead. "Are you sure about all that? There are really flowers and kittens?"

"Yes. That's where I live. It's a place with cute babies and motherly love. I may still smell a little like my mom. You want to sniff?" Pete held out his hand, and Gaug retreated quickly. Emboldened, Pete continued. "I just want to go back there. If I get the bone from you, you'll get it back. All that I get out of the deal is that I get to go home, and you get to stay here where you like it."

"Where's Bones now?"

Pete hesitated. He knew he'd left Bones at Cyril's house. Pete hated to think what Gaug might do to Cyril or his house, but the only way to get past Gaug was to tell him where to find Bones. "The last time I saw him, he was at Cyril's playing a card game. I don't know if he's still there, but I'm sure he would like to answer any questions you have."

"Oh, I'll ask him some questions!" Gaug punched a nearby tree. The tree uprooted and flew ten feet into another tree, which then broke in half. "My bones are in my den. Just go right in and grab one. I'll go talk to Bones and see what he has to say for himself. Hurry up, kid! I can almost smell those flowers now!" Gaug shuddered before storming off toward Cyril's shanty, though his disgusting smell lingered behind.

Pete trudged toward Gaug's den, hoping Cyril would be okay. The cave loomed, dark and smelly over him. The wind blew, making a roaring sound against its entrance. Just inside, he spotted the pile of bones. He found a nice, solid femur bone. Finally, he had all the items. Hope warmed him. If he could manage to get back to Heikle before Benny, he will have saved the world.

When Pete stepped out of the cave, a familiar face, or lack thereof, waited. Benny. Pete's inner warmth turned ice cold. How had Benny escaped Gaug?

"Thought you had me there, didn't you? I was hiding three trees over from you. I heard everything you had to say. Who's trying to get who killed here? That's fine though. I just stopped by to tell you I have all my items too. So I guess it's just a matter of who gets to Heikle first, isn't it? Care for one last challenge? I'll race ya,'" Benny kicked a pile of dirt at Pete and ran.

Chapter Sixteen

Pete finally managed to open his eyes. Small grits of dirt still irritated them, but he shook it off and ignored the pain. He had to catch up with Benny.

He turned onto the dirt path and ran as hard as he could. He passed Cyril's shanty, which Gaug had nearly torn apart while searching for Benny. His chest tightened with guilt. Cyril was the only true friend he had met in the graveyard. Now his home was in shambles.

He passed Hilda's hut, which had a freshly patched wall. In the distance was the fork that led to Melvin and Mervin's Ponds. He rushed past Dusty, who was feeding a flock of crows with corn kernels.

The scarecrow yelled, "Look at all my new friends!"

But Pete had to keep running. There was no time to lose. Just ahead, he saw Benny, who was still running. But he was within reach.

Pete ran as hard as his legs and lungs would allow. All the years of watching television and playing video games had sapped him of his childhood energy.

Benny turned and saw Pete. He tipped his hat in a mocking gesture and tripped over a rock. His bones loudly clapped together as he fell. He rolled and rolled until finally, he came to a stop. He was just a heap of bones and clothing.

Pete continued to run. His ribs ached, and his lungs and legs burned. He was weak all over and wheezing. Just as he passed the pile that was Benny, a hard, bony hand grabbed his ankle. He fell to the ground, which knocked the little air he had out of his lungs. He was exhausted, but he had to fight Benny off and get back up, no matter what. The fate of the world was up to him. With the femur from Gaug's den, he knocked Benny's hand away with a loud *clack*.

"Ouch!" Benny said, yet he still clung to Pete's ankle.

"Let go of me, Benny!"

"Not a chance! You think I'm going to let you, the grandkid of the punk who beat me all those years ago, beat me? No way! Get used to the idea, kid. I'm going to win this time!"

Pete furiously beat Benny's hand until Benny let go. Pete climbed to his feet. His legs were like rubber. He had never run so much in his life. *Come on!* Pete urged his body. *Just a little further!*

Benny's bones rolled around, clacking back into place, one after another. After he got to his feet, he limped past Pete, who was still pathetically wobbling around.

"See ya, loser. I'll make sure to give you plenty of thanks in my acceptance speech." Benny laughed.

Pete kept pace with Benny, who favored one ankle. They were a pathetic pair. Both determined to beat the other to Heikle, who stood a mere fifteen feet away.

Benny pushed Pete. Pete pushed back. Both grunted and groaned.

Heikle was so close, yet he might as well have been a mile away. Pete could barely get his bearings. He gritted his teeth and summoned every tiny bit of energy left in his body. *Only another ten feet to go.* He quickened his steps. Benny kicked Pete's foot out from under him, and Pete fell face-first and landed with a hard *thud*. He crawled as Benny hobbled further away.

"No!" Pete cried.

But it was too late. Benny had made it to Heikle. He turned around with his skeletal arms in the air. "I can't believe it! Finally, finally, I won!"

Pete crawled the rest of the way to Heikle, who was nearly eye-level with him.

"Not so fast, Bones," chided Heikle. "I must first assess the items collected. I will start with the presumed runner-up. Pete Davidson, please present the items you collected."

Pete handed them over. One by one, Heikle assessed and appraised them. "Twig from the nearest bush, a straw from Dusty's head, a strand of seaweed from Melvin's pond, a hair from a pig's tail from Hilda's hut—" Heikle read each entry with more enthusiasm than the last. But Pete felt no solace. What difference did it make? Benny had made it to Heikle first. "—a blue-flamed lantern from Cyril's shanty, and a bone from Gaug's scrap pile!" Heikle smiled. "Amazing job, young man."

"Thanks," Pete mumbled.

"Now, for the presumed winner." Heikle stretched out a hand.

Benny emptied his pockets. Among several non-list things, like a furry, brown spider and an orange and black salamander, he found all of the items from his list and handed them over.

Heikle examined each closely, saying with his high-pitched voice, "Yes," after each correct item. He reached the sixth item and hesitated. "Wait!"

Benny tilted his head. A faint glimmer of hope resonated in Pete. Had Benny not completed his list?

"I'm not finding a spade, Benny."

"Oh, well that's simple. The spades are in the deck of cards."

"Benny, none of these cards have spades. Every one of them is red. There are hearts and diamonds, but there are no spades."

"Just give them a minute, I tell you! They will change to spades at any second! Watch!"

Pete could hardly contain his excitement. There was a real chance of winning now.

Just then, Cyril came by. "Hey, folks. How are the lists coming along?"

"Cyril!" yelled Benny. "Tell Heikle about the cards. Tell them how they change suits. At any moment, they will change to spades, right?"

"Oh, Bones, I'm so sorry. I think I got the decks mixed up. I have the enchanted cards here with me." Cyril pulled a deck of cards from his pocket. He fanned them out. The suits changed, one after the other.

"What? You mean you gave me a deck that had no spades whatsoever? You cheated me! Whose side are you on?"

"As I said, it was an accident. I'm very sorry." Cyril winked at Pete. "Oh, and one more thing. Apparently Gaug wants to talk to you about something. He muttered something about kittens, flowers and butterflies. I don't know what he means. You'll have to ask him yourself."

Heikle's tiny face reddened. "If you folks don't mind, I have a contest to judge here! After considering both entrants lists and items, I have no choice other than to declare young Mr. Pete Davidson the winner."

Pete was elated. He had won, due to Cyril. He didn't know how to thank him. Perhaps by keeping the two worlds apart, he had repaid him enough. But still, Pete didn't want to leave without telling Cyril how much he appreciated his help.

"Bones!" A terrible voice rumbled. It was Gaug. He charged at Benny. Benny tried to limp away, but Gaug gained on him fast.

"Now it is time for you to go," said Heikle.

"But wait, I didn't get to thank Cyril yet!"

"You just did," said Cyril. "Now get out of here. Live your life to the fullest. Be happy."

Cyril and Heikle faded away. In the distance, Benny faded, as did Gaug, who had nearly caught up with the skeleton.

Pete blinked a couple of times. He was surrounded by crumbled headstones. The wrought-iron fence was back. He turned, and there was his grandparents' house!

Chapter Seventeen

Pete looked around. Everything seemed back to normal. He picked up his drawing pad. All the art was still intact, just as he'd left it. He thumbed through the pictures. His monster truck, his dinosaur, the portrait of his father, it was all there.

But there was something new. It was a picture of the giant graveyard. Cyril, Heikle, Hilda, Dusty, Mervin, and Gaug were all there. In the back, stood Benny. As always, he was dressed in his hat and suit, but judging by his body language, he was angry.

Pete knew he was mad about being beaten yet again.

"You made it back!" A deep voice nearly caused Pete to drop his artwork again.

He turned. His papaw stood outside the wrought-iron fence with his arms crossed, looking looked angry.

"I'm not surprised, really," Papaw said. "You are a Davidson, after all. I'm just a little upset you went against my wishes and went in there anyhow. I guess you found out why I told you it was dangerous."

"I'm sorry. I had no idea. I saw my drawings, and I wanted to grab them before they blew away. And ... hey, wait a minute! Why didn't you just tell me about Benny and the giant graveyard? Why didn't you tell me about the scavenger hunt? I might have been killed! For that matter, the world as we know it could've ended!"

Papaw lowered his head. "I know I should've. I really, really should've, and I'm sorry I didn't. But I thought you'd think I was making up wild stories. Then I thought those wild stories might draw you to the graveyard instead of keeping you out. That, in my mind, was worse than telling you the truth."

"You're probably right. I might've gotten bored at some point and come into the graveyard anyway, especially if you would've told me about Benny. He was still mad about the fact you outsmarted him." Pete chuckled.

"So you forgive me, then?

"Of course I do! I'm the one who should apologize."

"Well, you're home now. That's what's important. Come on. Let's get away from here." Papaw opened the screeching gate, and Pete left the graveyard, relieved to see it from the outside and not from within.

"That Benny will know better than to mess with us Davidson's anymore, huh?" said Pete.

Papaw laughed. "Yeah, I'd say you're right. Your dad must have raised you well."

"Yeah, I guess he has. Hey, why is it you still live by it? I mean, why haven't you moved? Right now, I just want to get as far away from it as possible. It seems like it would be safer that way."

"Well, I thought about it when I first beat Benny. But even if I was unable to stop you, it's my responsibility to keep people away from it. When I told your folks we didn't want you here, it wasn't because we don't love you, because we do. It's just too dangerous to be here without someone watching the graveyard."

That explained why his grandparents never went anywhere. They never went to birthday parties or Christmas get-togethers. They'd never visited to see him growing up. It was all because they had a more important purpose—they were keeping the graveyard under a close guard. They wanted to make sure there would never be another scavenger hunt under their watch.

Pete and his papaw shared an awkward silence. Pete wanted to hug his papaw, but they barely knew each other. "So," Papaw broke the silence, "you wanna go scare your mamaw?"

"You know I do!"

Pete and his papaw laughed.

"Well, let's go inside then. Maybe I can find some more of that milk you like so much."

"Bleh, no thanks!"

Papaw laughed again. They left the graveyard behind and made their way to the house. But before they made it to the porch, a strange humming sounded overhead and a blinding light flashed down on them. They shielded their eyes and looked up. It was too bright to see. Pete clung to his papaw in fear.

The light narrowed from a wide circle to a narrow one highlighting them. Within moments, they were lifted from the ground. Pete's stomach felt weightless, like when he used to ride the roller coasters at Kentucky Kingdom.

"What's going on?" Pete clamped his mouth shut when the urge to throw up claimed him.

"I have no idea! This is something new!" Papaw answered.

Suddenly, the light was gone and Pete and Papaw were on a solid, metallic surface. Pete knocked on the floor, and it responded with a hollow *clang*. A large screen, like a giant television, came on. A strange colorful snow filled it. A green glow lit the room. The walls were a strange framework of metal lined with lights. A figure came onto the screen. It was a strange-looking sort of thing with four bulbous eyes, a tiny mouth, small slits in place of a nose, and two winding antennae on its head. It looked like an alien from an old black and white movie.

"Greetings, Orville and Pete Davidson." The strange creature spoke with an almost bug-like voice. "We have longed to meet you, Orville. But now that Pete has proved himself worthy, we decided to bring you both along."

"Who are you?" Papaw asked with a shaky voice.

"My name is of no importance at the moment. As I said, we have been watching you for some time now. A decision has been made. You will be the next in line for our intergalactic scavenger hunt."

"What? No, not again!" Pete cried.

From the Author

Thank you for buying my little book. Here's hoping it provided you a few hours of entertainment and that you'll look for future stories in the NightScares series.

It is my goal to have many before I call it quits. In the meantime, do me a favor and spread a little NightScares spirit to your friends and neighbors. Tell your own scary stories and play practical jokes. You only have one childhood after all.

Stay scary and be sure to sleep with the lights on!

~Brian Barnett

About Brian Barnett

Brian Barnett is the author of over two hundred short stories and poems that have been published in dozens of books. He lives in Frankfort, Kentucky with his wife, Stephanie, and his children, Michael, Sebastian and Jane.

26650057R00054

Made in the USA
San Bernardino, CA
02 December 2015